The Jerusalem 14

...heresy of the highest accord

Hosanna, hosanna
The Jerusalem fourteen,
The story of a desert white boy,
12 Zealots and their queen.

The desert white boy Jesus,
The man called Nazarene,
Could lay down his rap
Smooth and pristine.

Scouted by Judas,
A recruiter for Zealots,
Judas who stood in awe
Of the devotion Jesus got.

Words of peace from Jesus
Judas did not want to hear.
Judas wanted Jesus to preach
Of the sword and the spear.

So Judas talked to Jesus,
But Jesus would not budge;
Jesus was a man of peace,
Unlike Romans held no grudge.

Judas reported to Mary
And Judas told his boss,
"Check out the desert white boy,
Or it will be your loss."

Now at that time in the holy land,
Many talked the talk,
Some dressed the part,
And some they walked the walk.

Many claimed to be
King of the Jews,
But Mary had heard of Jesus
By word of mouth news.

So Mary went to see Jesus,
And she was truly amazed
At the size of his following
And the way they sang his praise.

And because Jesus was so peaceful
The Romans ignored their ban
On large public assemblies;
The guards acted like his fans.

But Mary and her Zealots
Experienced the Romans in action,
And the desert white boy Jesus
They could use as a distraction.

Mary of the Zealots
Suddenly smiled and snapped her thumb.
"I'll knock over the money changer vaults
Under holy Jerusalem."

So Mary of the Zealots
Told Judas to pick 11 men,
To gather to break bread with her,
To plan the Jerusalem break in.

At supper Mary showed her Zealots
How they had the skills required
To rob Jerusalem's money changer vaults
And live out their lives retired.

Of the temples Roman guard,
In order to pull the job,
The desert white boy Jesus
Would provide an angry mob.

Said Judas,
"The desert white boy Jesus will never go along."
"Yes he will," said Mary,
Lifting her robe to reveal her thong.

The 12 bare witnessed and knew
Jesus need not join:
Surely no man on earth
Could refuse Mary's juicy loin.

So Mary went to meet Jesus
At a wine fish fry jamboree,
Sponsored by the Roman guard
Who were giving out fish for free.

When the desert white boy Jesus
Saw Mary step from the crowd
He was taken by her beauty,
And bent his knee and bowed.

And Jesus said to Mary,
Holding back his wad,
"One has but to look at you
To know there is a god."

The desert white boy Jesus,
One not to play at games,
Curled Mary close in his arms and asked,
"Tell me what's your name?"

Mary smiled at Jesus,
Muscularly delicious to her eyes.
She licked her lips slowly,
Thinking of his groin and thighs.

"Close friends call me Mary,
But you call me Mary Magdalene."
And so fell the desert white boy,
Smitten by the Zealot queen.

Caught were Jesus and Mary
In a whirlwind of romance,
Spending days then weeks together,
Making love at every chance.

And Mary said to Jesus,
"Caiaphas is back from Rome.
Alas my love I'm leaving,
It's time I must go home."

The desert white boy Jesus
Turned to Mary and said,
"I don't like you leaving;
Mary Magdalene we must wed."

"Then come with me to Jerusalem
To be blessed by the high priest,
Tell all of your followers
My father will throw a feast."

"It's not quite that simple,
I will loose my cool.
First fire, now money, words and temples,
They are worshiping their tools.

If I reflect that anger
My followers will mob,
And the temple is guarded by Romans
Eager to do their job."

"Come with me to Jerusalem,
The high priest is my dad
I know he will like you."
But Jesus just grew sad.

"Caiaphas is your father,
Caiaphas is the man,
Iron clad establishment,
I don't dig that plan."

"Come with me to Jerusalem,"
Mary began to cry,
"You said you are my soul mate."
Tears welled in her eyes.

"Come with me to Jerusalem,
We will marry so you said,
We will be together forever,
We will always share our bed.

Come with me to Jerusalem,
To be husband and wife.
Come with me to Jerusalem,
For I carry a new life."

And Jesus said to Mary,
"That's all you had to say;
I love you Mary Magdalene,
Pick a time place and day."

And Mary said to Jesus,
"I will go on ahead
To Jerusalem to tell father."
And Mary leapt from bed.

Then Mary sent word to Judas
That Jesus was under her thumb.
So readied the 12 Zealots,
For operation Jerusalem.

Mary went home to Jerusalem
To her house behind its walls,
Home to the holy temple,
Home to imperial halls.

Caiaphas was in his chamber,
Writing the scripture's meat,
When burst in Mary his daughter,
Falling to the high priest's feet.

"Helena Miriam Caiaphas-Magdalene,
What is the meaning of this?
What is of such importance?
What is it you think I will miss?"

And Mary asked her father,
Her face flushed with joy,
"Have you herd of Jesus,
Jesus the desert white boy?"

"Yes I've heard of Jesus,
Of his effect on the crowd.
A powerful peaceful presence,
A peasant in the clouds.

Yes I've heard of Jesus,
The Romans send reports.
Definitely not a Zealot,
A cult leader of some sorts.

Yes I've heard of Jesus.
I've heard Jesus is coming,
I've heard Jesus is the one,
I've heard about your slumming.

Your dirty white boy plaything
Will have his skin whipped raw.
You will marry Herod's son
According to our law."

"Father I love Jesus,
Our love is not obscene.
Please show Jesus mercy,
Why are you so mean?"

"Running around with a peasant,
At least he could be black!
The desert white boy Jesus!
Guards hold me back!"

"Father I love Jesus,
Bless us so we can wed.
Love can not be preordained,
Marry me to Jesus instead."

"You and a desert white boy,
You can give up that hope,
Rather you just hanged me now.
Guards get me some rope!"

"Father I love Jesus,
Jesus with all my heart.
Say we can stay together,
Do not keep us apart."

"Apart?

Alone in the desert with a white boy,
What will people think?
Tell me you are still a virgin.
Guards get me drink!"

"Father I love Jesus,
Loving Jesus is not a sin.
I miss being curled in Jesus' arms,
I long to be with Jesus again."

"Helena what are you saying?
No, I don't want to hear,
Spare me the lurid details.
Guards cover your ears!"

"No I am not a virgin,
And I was not defiled,
For I am in love with Jesus.
Father, I carry Jesus' child."

Caiaphas looked down at Mary.
He said, "This is so unfair;
The desert white boy Jesus.
Marry him, I don't care."

"I love you father," yelped Mary
Jumping to her feet.
She kissed Caiaphas and said,
"I can't wait until you meet."

So the Temple sent word to Jesus
To come to break bread,
His followers would be welcome,
His followers would be fed.

And Caiaphas sent word to Jesus,
That at the engagement feast,
They would talk father to son,
And not peasant to high priest.

Jesus was on the highway
When Jesus received the word.
Jesus cried, "Hallelujah!"
And for miles his voice was heard.

And the word spread like fire,
By word of mouth news,
About the high priest's daughter
And the desert white boy muse.

Jesus was on the highway
When joined him 12 Zealot men,
And Jesus said to Judas,
"It's good to see friends again."

By the time they reached Jerusalem,
Jesus followers already had arrived,
And Jesus stood exulted
By Romans helping the deprived.

Jesus and the 12 Zealots
Went 13 separate ways:
12 to rob the money changer vaults,
And Jesus to the temple to pray.

Then Jesus went to find Mary
In her temple home,
In her lap of luxury
Beneath the golden dome.

When Jesus found Mary's chambers
A eunuch by the door,
Said "Jesus you are early,
We break bread at four.

Go back to your followers,
Go find your 12 Zealot friends.
Helena is in her bath with maids,
It's best you not go in."

Said Jesus "My Mary Magdalene,
When she sees me will be glad,
And dripping wet bathing beauties,
Trust me, is never bad."

But Jesus wasn't invited
To Mary's private feast,
And the eunuchs knew Helena Miriam Caiaphas-Magdalene,
None of them the least.

Jesus went into Mary's bath,
Few know what Jesus saw.
"Mary Magdalene," Jesus screamed,
"That acts against god's law."

Jesus was playing his part,
Mary had set the stage.
Jesus ran out of Mary's bath,
Consumed by godlike rage.

Jesus ran from Mary's chambers,
Out into the temples courtyard,
Jesus ran eyes tearing,
Into two temple Roman guards.

Jesus and the two Romans
Fell forcibly to the ground,
Fellow temple Roman guards
Turned to site the sound.

Reacting, the temple Roman guards
Built a wall with their shields
Between Jesus and his followers,
And shouted at Jesus to yield.

The temple courtyard was packed,
Jesus followers were wall to wall,
Many had heard the word,
Many witnessed Jesus fall.

The Centurion Barabbas,
Realizing who Jesus was,
Shouted "Sheath gladius, batons."
And to Jesus said, "Sorry cuz."

But 12 Zealots amongst the crowd
Were waiting for a queue,
And seeing Jesus surrounded,
They knew just what to do.

"The Romans have killed Jesus,"
The 12 Zealots began to shout.
The Jesus followers carried the cry,
And then all hell broke out.

The Roman wall stood fast,
As the mob futilely attacked.
"Get Jesus inside," Barabbas cried
While beating Jesus followers back.

Barabbas ordered his century
To toss temple coins into the sands.
Jesus' followers stopped rioting,
But fought on their knees and hands.

As Mary had predicted,
Jesus provided an angry mob.
The 12 Zealots got in and got out,
Pulling off the Jerusalem job.

Many nations had fallen
To gladius and Roman will,
But Barabbas performed a miracle
Roman order with no one killed.

Yet Jerusalem's underground vaults,
The Zealots had robbed all the same,
And the money changers went to Caiaphas,
Blaming the desert white boy by name.

Desperately the high priest called in
All of the favors he could,
But it was Jesus or the money,
And the Zealots had taken the goods.

So Caiaphas had to tell Helena,
There was nothing he could do or say,
The situation was out of his hands,
And Jesus would die the next day.

Mary cried alone in despair,
Sitting in her private temple yard.
"Hail Mary," said Barabbas
Centurion of the temple Roman guard.

Barabbas handed Mary a scroll,
"From Jesus," Barabbas said.
Crying Mary slowly read it,
Whimpering Mary went to bed.

By the Romans Jesus was arrested,
By the Romans Jesus was tried,
By the Romans Jesus was convicted,
By the Romans Jesus was crucified.

Jesus remembered on the cross,
Centurion Barabbas shout,
"It's a drink of wine and vinegar."
Then darkness and blacking out.

A gull cried in the air,
White clouds, a blue sky,
Mary's beautiful smile,
And Jesus said, "Where am I?"

And Mary said to Jesus,
"On a ship at sea.
The Zealots rescued you my love,
They would do anything for me.

For I am Helena,
Helena Miriam Caiaphas-Magdalene,
I am the high priest of Jerusalem's daughter,
I am the Zealot queen."

And although Helena's father Caiaphas
Died the laughing stock of town,
In the end the high priest came out on top,
He wrote the whole story down.

Hosanna, hosanna
The Jerusalem eighteen:
The desert white boy Jesus, 13 Zealots, and Mary,
A very pregnant Zealot queen.

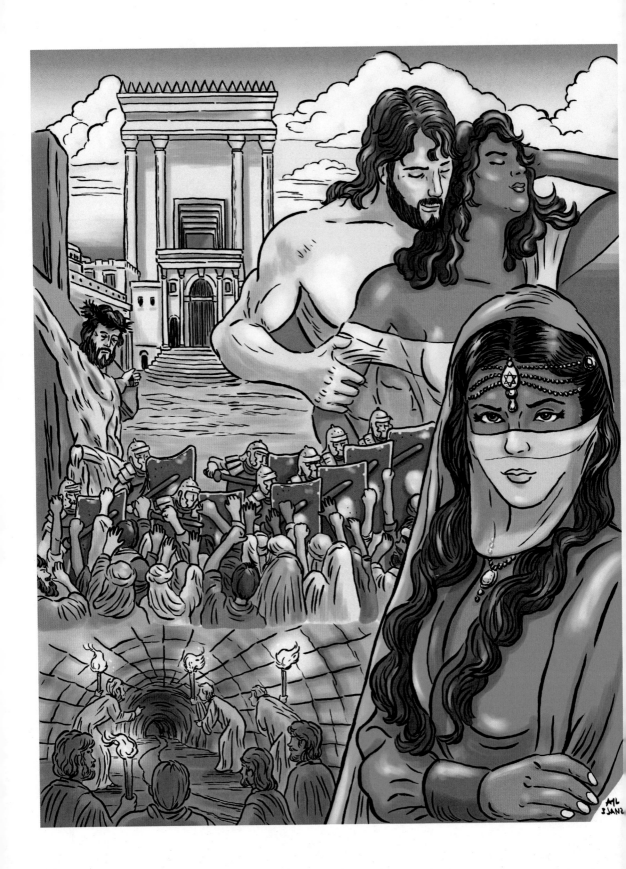

About the Author

Carlton Lewis Sampson

Carlton Lewis Sampson, a poet and graphic novel author produced two other publications in collaboration with two different artists. *Po Lyn Lee; Ophelia House* is a horror fiction fantasy about belief and social class, illustrated by Andrew L. Willis. *Phascist Clowns; D.I.T.O. Live!*, a political fiction fantasy warning of consolidated wealth, is illustrated by Chris Robinson. Carlton Lewis Sampson's books are available online at carltonlewissampson.com and amazon.com.

Po Lyn Lee; Ophelia House

When Grandmother, majesty of a secret sisterhood, sends Po, her trained she demon, a message to assassinate the president of the United States, Po's incidental romantic encounter with an artist leads Po to question Grandmother's messages and reject her conditioned demonic behavior. Po, a cannibal, realizing she is a demon, struggles with self-awareness, self-discovery, and humanity amidst the glamour, intrigue, espionage and morality of the global elite. Illustrated by Andrew L. Willis, *Po Lyn Lee; Ophelia House*, is a horror fiction fantasy about social class, and a 574-page, full color, graphic novel published as 12 single chapter issue comic books and as a volume, available online at polynlee.com and amazon.com.

Phascist Clowns; D.I.T.O. Live!

The Phascist Clowns are the members of the Circus, descendants of interconnected families controlling the key natural resources and organizations with the majority of influence over the billions of socialites (people) living on the planet Socia. When Circus member Heir Head, global leader of industry, visits one of his top-secret munitions facilities to witness the testing of a new weapon system, he encounters mayhem and terrorism, symptoms of the social extremes caused by the Circus. Illustrated by Chris Robinson, *Phascist Clowns; D.I.T.O. Live!* is a political fiction fantasy warning of consolidated wealth, and a 28-page black and white comic book available online at phascistclowns.com and amazon.com.

About the Illustrator

Alexander T. Lee

Alexander T. Lee was born in Philadelphia and currently resides in Chalfont, Pennsylvania, with his wife Yu Yuan and their son Julian and daughters Caitlyn and Kara. He graduated from the University of Arts with a Bachelors in Fine Arts in Illustration. After graduation, he enlisted in the US Navy and served four years on the submarine, USS Jacksonville, as a computer technician. After he completed his service with the US Navy, he began to pursue his lifelong dream of illustrating children's books. He furthered his studies at Delaware County Community College with an Associate in Applied Science in Graphic Design.

He now works as a freelance illustrator and designer and continues to incorporate all of his experiences and skills into his works that can be found at alextlee.com.

Made in the USA
Middletown, DE
23 June 2023

32961341R10027